I0730967

C. MURPHY

EMPIRE OF LIONS

REAMS OF A DIFFERENT KIND OF LIFE
SAGA 1

WORKBOOK PRESS LLC
187 E Warm Springs Rd,
Suite B285, Las Vegas, NV 89119, USA

Website: https://workbookpress.com/
Hotline: 1-888-818-4856
Email: admin@workbookpress.com

Ordering Information:
Quantity sales. Special discounts are available on quantity purchases by corporations, associations, and others.
For details, contact the publisher at the address above.

Library of Congress Control Number:
ISBN-13:   978-1-955459-74-7 (Paperback Version)
                978-1-955459-75-4 (Digital Version)

REV. DATE: 08/06/2021

Empire of Lions:

Dreams of a Different Kind of Life

Saga 1

By: C. Murphy

Dedication of Empire of Lions

This is a way of acknowledging those who have helped me along the way.

To my grandfather, Henry Murphy, Miss Naomi Boyd, my brother Hosea L. Mims, Jr., my loving sister Renee Mims, my brother Carlton Douglas Mims, I owe you all a lot since the beginning until now.

To my daughter Naomi Arndt, my son-in-law Ed, my son, Enoch, to my grandson Nathan, my son Enoch and to my loving daughter, Latriece, you all have been a big help, thank you very much.

Sharing my novel has allowed me to reflect on how far I've come to inspire more people to look always at the brighter side of life and to look forward for great stories.

And also the fact that I have been supported by the very best, to whom I can only say a truly heartfelt thank you.

DISCLAIMER: *The characters, names, locations, events, and incidents are purely fictional. Any resemblance to persons living or dead, locations and events are entirely coincidental.*

About the Author

C. Murphy was born in Utica, NY. She was born on September 16, 1948. She also retired in 2010, has three children: two daughters, one son, and a grandson.

She currently resides in Upstate, NY. She has 16 brothers and sisters and 16 siblings who are in-laws. One of her daughters is married and the other currently stays with her. She is 72 years old. C. Murphy is widowed.

<u>Empire of Lions</u>

Introduction

Empire of Lions tells the saga of a black scientist and his efforts to save himself and his friends from slow genocide and annihilation by a hostile society on earth. A black kid named Devon Wellings began to look toward the stars for escape from this horrendous situation. The tragic deaths of his mother and sister impacted him horribly, but it was the death of his best friend that drove him to find the answers he sought. The first saga (one in a series of many) will begin with the stories of two women who became friends and who were influential in the two boys' lives. The women were strong enough to survive some of the struggles and hopelessness that surrounded the women.

Eventually, the brutality of their lives will claim the women as well as most of the women in the boys' lives. When violence claims Devon's best friend, it leaves a profound effect on him and he is wounded emotionally and this latest trauma forces him to look for an answer to his anguish. Subsequent novels will explore the challenges that Devon and his small band will face, as they embark on a determination to escape the genocide and annihilation that is slowly creeping upon them.

Empire

<u>Empire of Lions</u>

Evansville, Indiana was a small slice of African-American life. Within the eastern part of the city was an area with a cast of players that occupied this strife-ridden part of the city. Its inhabitants found solace and comfort in the familiarity of each other within a huge radius that contained black people.

The Brighton Avenue Apartments comprised a huge area the size of three football fields. In 1983, things had not gotten much better for the people of the Brighton Street area. Despite the riots and the Civil Rights era unrest, things for the Brighton Street area didn't advance much. The young people were getting into trouble forming gangs, an Environment of Anguish and Hopelessness and selling drugs. They ending were also trapped in cycles of violence and prostitution and early deaths. Police descended almost daily in the area.

The residents had become accustomed to the daily sounds of gunfire, screams, and the often steady barrage of funerals that occurred as a result of the violence. The Brighton Avenue complex served as a dark and colossal reminder of the hopelessness and despair that plagued the area. Single mothers and their children inhabited this area. Many of the children never knew their fathers. Many of the fathers were incarcerated in the Evansville Penitentiary system, a state prison about twenty miles from Evansville.

<u>An Environment of Anguish and</u>

<u>Hopelessness</u>

Other fathers were dead. Most of Evansville are black men who went through a revolving door. They were lifestyles that led from a life of crime to violence. It led to prison resulting in an early death for the career for the career criminals who chose that tragic way of life. Among the many women who were abandoned by the men who once loved them were a young woman named Nadina Wellington. She was a single 18-year-old mother of a 3-year-old daughter named Remiah Turness. Nadina had gotten pregnant at fifteen. Her boyfriend at the time was Ben Turness, an 18-year-old street hustler who cared about anyone and/or anything.

He was not committed to fatherhood when he found out that Nadina was pregnant. He disappeared. Ben left Nadina and her mother to face Nadina's impending motherhood alone. When Lena Mae Hendrickson found out that her daughter was pregnant, she was furious and became enraged. "See, I told you that he wasn't no good!" She screamed at Nadina. "Still." "You were hard-headed and you refused to listen!" She continued. Lena Mae was furious at Nadina because she too, was a victim of a man's false love and promises, with its treachery and betrayal.

She wanted more for her daughter than the life that she had. Lena wanted Nadina to escape the brutality and hopelessness of the Brighton Street Area complex. She was deeply disappointed in the mistake Nadina had made. She didn't hide her resentment and unhappiness from the rest of their neighbors, who were nosy and who wanted something to gossip about. They wasted no time in making a bad situation worse. Gossiping about Nadina's pregnancy usually added aggravation and isolated Lena and Nadina. One of those neighbors who lives across the hall from Nadina and her mother was a woman whose name was Millie Mae Hommers, who had moved into the three room apartment. Millie Mae was the elder of the three women. Also living at the end of the hall at the western end of the building was Herbert and Justine Simon's son. Many other residents lived on various floors throughout the complex. Many other residents were criminals or living with other boyfriends who were criminals.

Some African-American males were fortunate enough to find employment. If the young black males stayed in school and were fortunate to finish high school or were fortunate enough to get two years of college, they would find good jobs. These men who were few and far between, made good money and married young women who had college degrees and got good jobs. Within three years these successful people moved away. These families with their children did well.

They were the exception. The majority they left behind were not as fortunate. Most of the children ran the streets of Evansville. They soon embarked on a life of crime. When they were hungry, they stole food to eat and clothing to wear if they weren't caught. A young man along with a small cluster of people along with him would try and save themselves from the slow genocide that was creeping up on them.

Back at the apartment, Remiah was complaining about Millie Mae being so mean. Millie Mae admonished Remiah about some remark the little girl had made. "Be quiet, Remiah." "You are not grown yet." Remiah's grandmother retorted. Nadina longed for some women her own age for friendship and for some companionship. Most of the young women her age were in school or graduating from some of the academic programs. Justine Simonson remained aloof from the women. She could be heard yelling at Herbert for some small infraction concerning a woman. Justine 's behavior had created many enemies in the complex for her.

The first of many tragedies hit Nadina suddenly. It caused her to become unhappy and bitter. Nadina had gone to work at the Brisdale Market. Her father came by the apartment. Lena Mae hated Nadina's father. The fact that he had to pay child's support didn't improve the relationship between them. Paying seventeen years of child support didn't improve the relationship between the two of them.

On this day an argument ensued between the man and his former girlfriend. Suddenly Aniston Wellington pulled out a gun and shot Lena Mae. She was dead before she hit the floor. "Grandmomma, grandmomma"! Remiah screamed. Nadina's father pushed Remiah out of his way when he rushed out of the doorway of the Brighton Apartments. Amidst all of the commotion Hebert rushed out of his apartment and scooped up Remiah and handed the crying little girl over to Millie Mae, the across-the-hall neighbor. Other residents were coming out of their apartments. One woman screamed upon seeing blood and Lena Mae's dead body. Herbert quickly shut the door to Lena's apartment.

It was 5 o'clock pm Tuesday afternoon in August 1985. Nadina was on her way home and had not heard the tragic news about her mother. It was beginning to break out on news and radio stations throughout the area. As Nadina rounded the corner leading into the Brighton Street area, flashing red lights on Emergency Police Vehicles, gave her a sickening feeling in the pit in her stomach. She quickly retraced her steps to the complex. Nadina ran up the stairs that led to the entrance way of the complex. She went to the inside of the building. Nadina took the elevator to the 4th floor. As the elevators opened the coroner's response team wheeled Nadina's lifeless body past her and to the coroner's van. The smell of death as in the elevator. Nadina could not say anything. She was numb.

Herbert came down the hall "C'mon Dena, something has happened to ya mamma." "We have to go and identify her," he quietly said. Herbert was going to do everything he could to assist Nadina in her time of sorrow. After the identification was completed, a sobbing Nadina was helped home. "Thanks, Herb". She sobbed through tears. Herb said quietly "don't you think about nothin'. Everything's gonna be just fine."

They went back to the complex. Nadine found the police waiting for her. Inside the apartment, her mother and daughter shared with Lena Mae, the large pool of blood emitted a dark and somber mood in the apartment. The sun slowly setting made everything look even darker. The day was a long one. Herbert, Justine, and Millie Mae stayed with Nadina and Remiah. Justine and Millie Mae set about cleaning the rug and the floor. The two detectives and one police officer began to talk to Nadine.

They had pads in their hands. "My name is Detective John Mastos", the black haired handsome detective said. "My partner's name is Bren McDooge." His brown hair and eyes told a sadness in the work he had to do. Detective Mastos asked Nadina, "What is your father's name." Nadina quietly replied. Detective Mastos continued. "When did you see him last?" Nadina said "I can't remember." He then asked, "Where were you." Nadina said, "I was at work." What's the name and where is it at?" The detective continued. Nadina was becoming confused. "I work at the Brisdale Market at 415 Brisdale Avenue, why are you asking me all these questions?" Nadina asked a hint of annoyance in her voice. "I am investigating a murder, Miss Wellings." The tone of his voice became conciliatory and apologetic.

Herbert was becoming annoyed as well. They then turned to him. "Who are you?" They asked him. Herbert said "I'm a neighbor. I live in the apartment down the hall."   That's my wife Justine over there." Detective Mastos continued. "Did you know the suspect?" Detective Mastos asked. Herbert answered "No, I didn't know him that well. I heard of him but I never met him and with all the bad stuff I heard about him, I never wanted to meet him. The police talked with Nadina a long time into the late night.   They knew it was a case of a domestic killing. They, Herbert, Nadina and MIllie Mae took their cards and left. They radioed in a CPB ALL Points Bulletin for Aniston Wellings.

The apartment still reeked of blood and bleach. As Nadina cried herself to sleep in Remiah's room, Nadina tried to wonder why her father would kill her mother. Her mother did not speak well of her father, but the deep seated animosity did not present itself until earlier today. The next day, Nadina nearly overslept.

She forgot to turn the alarm clock on. She shook Remiah slightly awoke. Dina said "C'mon sweet pea, you gotta go to school." She gave Remiah her bath and got her dressed for school. She got her dressed and made Remiah some lunch.   She decided to call Brisdale Market. She still could smell the blood. As she dialed the number,

Dan Brisdale the owner spoke. "Hello, Dina started to talk. She sobbed into the receiver as she spoke. "I won't be in for a couple of days.

I have family problems. He quietly said, "You can take a week off, Nadina" He also said "Some Detectives asked about you." "I said nothing but good things about you." Dina said "Thank you, Mr. Brisdale."

Dina took Remiah downstairs to her classroom. Then she went and she knocked softly on Millie Mae's door. She opened the door cautiously. She said " C'mon in Dina." She walked in and sat down on the couch. Dina said " Thanks for cleaning the floor." Millie Mae replied, You're very welcome. That bastard, I hope they catch him. She was such a nice person. He didn't have to do that to her."

Another knock was at the door. Millie got up out of her chair. "I wonder who that is." she grumbled. When she opened the door, it was Herbert. She jokingly said "Don't Justine know where you at?" Herbert replied "She's gone to work" Herbert said to Nadina, "How you doin?'" She replied in a tired tone in her voice, "Okay, I guess. I hope they catch that son-of-a-bitch!" He didn't have to do that to Lena Mae." If I see him, I'm callin' the cops on him! Lena was such a nice person." The next few days were busy ones for Nadina and Remiah. Lena Mae had lost a lot of blood and even though the office had the maintenance crew clean up the apartment, it was not about the same legal issues about the lease that came up.

Nadina wanted another apartment.   Remiah and Nadina were afraid to live in the apartment, especially at night. Nadina was not eighteen years old, yet.   She didn't know what to do.   Nadina wanted another apartment. Remiah and Nadina were afraid to live in the apartment, especially at night. She didn't know what to do. Nadina had a part-time job. It would be a struggle to pay the bills and to pay the rent, but it could be done.   Herbert, Justine, and Millie Mae all stepped in to help. Since Nadina was not eighteen years old yet, she could not enter into any contracts. Herbert told Nadina that he could help her rent her mother's apartment. Nadina replied that she didn't want to rent her mother's apartment.

Nadina didn't know what to do. She and Remiah had nowhere to go. Herbert told Nadina that he would sublet an apartment in his name and when Nadina turned eighteen, she could rent the apartment in her own name. Since Nadine could not live anywhere right now and since no one else was helping her and Remiah, they had no choice but to take Herbert and Justine's offer.

"You'll have to get welfare if you lose that job. I ain't paying for rent." Nadine replied "I know." She clearly understood. She and Remiah was now on their own. She hoped she could ask them questions if she needed to. Gifts poured in from all over the buildings. Some neighbors asked "you the girl that lost her mother?" Nadina was grateful for the gifts that came pouring in. A lot of it being money and food. Millie Mae was invaluable in helping Nadina. Remia was crying about missing her grandmother. She knew her grandma wasn't coming back. There were funeral arrangements to make and talking to Lena's friends. It would take a lot out of Nadina.

She would soon be eighteen years old. Nadina had to mature emotionally and very quickly. And physically, because she was already a teen single mother. She was somewhat acclimated to the adult world anyway. Justine asked Nadina, "How are you holdin' up, girl?" "Ella Mae Timmonson sent some stuff for you and Remiah." Nadina answered "I'm okay." I began to cry in Nadine's arms. Justine said quietly, "It's alright, baby." Have they caught Tony yet?" Nadina said.

"No, but I do hope they catch him because I hate him so much for what he did to my mother!" The telephone rang and Nadine went over to pick up the receiver from the cradle off the phone. "She spoke softly." "Hello?" Yes, Miss Cooper, I'll be home." "Thank You." Nadina put the receiver back into its cradle. Justine asked Nadina "Was that Beatrice Cooper?" Nadina replied "Yeah," Nadina answered. Justine continued, "You better watch what you say to that woman." "I know about Miss Cooper." "She already stung me twice." She has something of mine and I want it!"

Nadina was slowly beginning to resent Justine's interference in her friendship with Beatrice. Nadine was after whatever gift she could get from Beatrice. Wednesday afternoon at 6 o'clock am in the morning, bought a late gathering of the Brighton Street residents in groups. They were getting ready to retire in their apartments for the evening. Like the birds going to roost, the residents had enough of the day. Two fights broke out between two women in the complex. The fights had escalated from the children to the women. Fists flew between the women as well as the name calling and threats of more violence. Herbert and Wesley Timmons' neighbor pulled the combatants apart. Herbert yelled at the women "you stop it!" "Y'all want the cops to come here and haul y'all asses off to jail?" The fighting stopped and the shouting and name calling began to subside.

Beatrice Cooper drove up in her 1985 tan colored Chevy 12 door Malibu. She parked in the parking lot of the back of the gigantic building complex. She looked around cautiously as she reached for the packaged chocolate cake and the potato salad for Nadina and Remiah. She had Known Lena Mae for a few years and wanted to pay her respects. Herbert came by from his weekly visit to the garbage room. He said "My, my, my, it smells good in here, Beatrice." Beatrice knew Herbert's tease the minute he started talking.

Beatrice asked Sly, "At it again ol' marble eyes?" Herbert replied "Ok, is that the way it is, huh?" He continued. "Keep up with that attitude and I won't open the door for you."   Beatrice answered, "Am I supposed to be upset?" Herbert teased her again. "Aw, come on, girl."   He winked at her. He did the gentlemanly thing for her and opened the door as well as pressed the button inside the elevator. The doors closed. The elevator stopped on the fourth floor.   They walked hand in hand up to Nadina's apartment.

Nadina had heard them coming and opened the door. "She said to them "Come on in." "I heard you talkin' in the hall." Beatrice was happy with herself. She had finished with high school and completed two years of college. It wasn't long before she landed a job at Evansville Consolidated Power Company. She was the only black female employed in her department. There were a few problems but because the supervisor had a black friend who was a school teacher, she helped Beatrice. The women who were giving her problems were transferred. Her eyes popped out when she saw her first paycheck. She had never seen that much money.   She worked two years and purchased a brand new car. She had many friends and looked out for her against the thugs who were eyeing her every move. She liked to come around Lena Mae just to show off her prosperity. She gave Lena Mae a few favors. She busied herself beyond Lena Mae's reach and wouldn't answer her.   Beatrice stayed a couple of hours then left Nadina's apartment. She was saddened by the fact that the police had not caught Tony yet. Herbert left Nadina's place as well. Nadina ran to the window. She could not see Herbert and Beatrice. She hoped Justine could not see them together. She quickly left the apartment and ran down the hall. She got on the elevator and when the elevator stopped, she got off quickly.

Nadina ducked out of sight so that they couldn't see her. She saw them walk to their cars. Herbert got into his car and Beatrice got into her car.   Both drove off. Herbert drove behind Beatrice. The general thought would be that Herbert was following Beatrice home. Nadina went back to her apartment. She was grateful for the $50 bucks, the chocolate cake, and the potato salad that Beatrice had given her and Remiah. Justine was not going to be happy with Herbert. She always knew that Herbert had a roving eye. Nadina hadn't believed it, but after what she saw, she was more willing to believe it.

"Girl,   what are you doin' in this hall?" Nadina asked. Remiah asked "Where have you been, momma?" Nadina shot back "Nevermind!" " You get back in the house!" Remiah at such a young age did not understand what her mother had done. Adulterous affairs in the black community were not spoken of around the children. They also turned a blind eye to the affairs. Nadina went through most of the gifts from the neighbors. It was much more to go before the gifts and cards were sorted through. She began to get Remiah ready for her bath and to put her to bed. There would be many more sad days to come.

On Saturday morning at 11 o'clock am, the service at the Williams Funeral Home was beginning. Nearly everyone in the Brighton Avenue Apts. attended Lena Mae's funeral. It was the worst day of Nadina's life. She didn't go, but she knew she and Remiah had to go. She wanted Herbert, Justine, and Millie Mae to ride in the hearse with her. Nadina noticed that Herbert and Justine weren't speaking to each other. She wondered if this situation was because of what happened the other day. Nadina hoped this new problem wouldn't bring anymore sadness to an already sad day.

Nadina couldn't believe all the people that came to her mother's funeral. All but a few of the residents hardly ever spoke to her. Beatrice came, then Nadine, Herbert, Justine, and Millie Mae.   Justine turned behind her and glared at Beatrice, and if she knew about what went on between her and her husband and whispered "Please come on Justine. This isn't the place or the time to settle any differences." Justine said nothing as they continued inside the funeral home.   "Another time, another place", Justine thought. As Nadine and Remiah and company took their place in the front row across from Lena Mae's casket, Nadina started to cry.

Justine consoled her Beatrice and couldn't look at Nadina. She seemed less friendly than the other evening. After what seemed like a longtime, the service concluded. The mourners walked out of the home behind the green casket.

After it was placed in the hearse, Justine waited to talk to a few people. When Beatrice came down the stairs and started on the side of the building, where she had parked her car, Justine quickly hurried behind her and pulled her hair. Justine shreked "You black bitch!" "You nasty ho!" I'm gonna beat your nasty ass!" Beatrice was caught off guard.

As the women fell to the ground, their dresses flew up. The

mourners gaped at the women, their mouths open. Herbert and another pallbearer pulled the two women apart. It was traumatic with all the yelling and name calling. Herbert grabbed his wife and pulled her apart from Beatrice. Another man pulled Beatrice apart from Justine. Berbert wrapped his arm around Justine's shoulders. He whispered calming words into her car.

After the altercation, the mourners went to their cars. Nadina was even more upset. When Justine got into the limousine, Nadina and Remiah were riding and Nadina yelled at Justine "Why did you make an already bad day worse?" She sat down across from Nadine and Remiah without saying a word. She had already had one fight today and she wasn't in the mood to have another. There wasn't a sound in the limousine as it followed Lena's hearse to Wooddale Cemetery.

As the hearse stopped at the third row at the end of the row, the hearse was lowered into the ground. The row was neat and clean. The mourners gathered quietly at the gravesite.   Tears flowed as the prayers were said. Justine hurried back to the limousine. Herbert hurried back as well. Nadine was glad that Justine and Bea didn't run into each other again. After Lena Mae was placed in the grave, flowers were placed in the grave.   So Nadina, after the funeral and burial of her mother, Nadina hated her father and never wanted to see him again. Remiah was told never to call him grandpa.

The mourners gathered at Nadina's apartment. There was business with the lease. Herbert said he'd help her with that as soon as she felt up to it. Most of the other mourners stood in small groups with their own stories about Lena Mae. They also talked about their own personal issues.

There was also so much food and money. Herbert, Millie Mae, and Justine kept track of the money since some of the local thugs had shown up for the gathering. There were gifts everywhere. People were coming up to Nadina and giving her stuffed envelopes full of cash. Herbert kept an eye on the gifts. The local thugs had shown up looking for easy pickins that wouldn't give them any trouble.

A tall young black male walked up to Nadina and Herbert. There were four other black males who were with him. "Sorry bout' yo moms," Cordell Langston said to Nadina. He had a gnarly grin that reminded Nadina of a snake. "Yeah, sure Cordell." Nadina said with an icy stare. Cordell was known as "Coke" because he was known to smoke more than Lena's Junkies. He made no bones about how he would get the money.

Usually, he would assault or rob someone particularly those who were afraid of him. Cordell's accomplice began to ramble among Nadina's belongings. "Hey, leave them things alone!" Millie Mae shouted at one of the thugs. "Shut the fuck up, you ol' bitch," one of the thugs hissed back. Nadina hurried to the front door and flung it open. The gesture signaled for Cordell and his gang of thugs to leave. "I'm kind of tired of Cordell so maybe you and your friends can leave." I'm going to bed." Nadina said. "Want some company, baby?" Cordell asked laughing out loud. He slowly glided past her as she turned her head.

Cordell and his friends moved slowly toward the door. To save face, he shouted to Nadina "Who do you think is making me leave?" You ain't makin' nobody else leave." Some of the other men in the room noticed the commotion. Herbert spoke up. "I heard that Det. Ralph Burman was lookin' for you, Cordell." "What did you do, now?" "None of yo' damn business ol' man." Stick to yo business and yo gonna live longer!" Cordell snapped.

One of the men near the window in the apartment said loudly, "Here come the cops right now and it looks like they're comin' this way!" Herbert was grateful for the statement Cordell and his gangster accomplices hurried past Nadina and quickly left the apartment.

Cordell and his accomplice ran down the hallway into the stairwell exit. Nadina closed the door, relieved that Cordell and his thugs had left. Herbert calmly   said "Somebody's gonna kill that boy one of these days" he continued. Then he said "I got to git me a piece."

It seemed like hours before the mourners left. Remiah began rubbing her eyes. She asked, "Is Cordell my daddy?" Nadina answered sternly to Remiah "Girl, please, I would have killed myself."   All kinds of things ran through Nadina's mind about Cordell, all of it bad. Nadina said "Come on Boo-it's bath time-I know you're tired, it's been a long day." After Remiah's bath, both mother and daughter went into Remiah's room. Remiah crawled into bed. She asked Nadina "Do you miss grandma?" Nadina answered "Yes, very much." She turned away from her daughter because she did not want to see her cry. After Remiah took her bath, it was nice and warm and soothing to Nadina. I didn't however keep her from crying herself to sleep. The next morning, Millie Mae stopped by. She asked Nadina, "How you holdin' up, girl?" Nadina replied softly, "I'm alright." I guess. I've been cryin' myself to sleep."   Millie Mae had only been in the apartment fifteen minutes before there was a loud knock at the door.

Nadina was as nervous as she thought that Cordell would return! She looked through the peephole in the door. The person outside the door was a white man with pepper colored hair. He held a badge up to the peephole. Another man was with him. A younger man with sandy colored hair was with him, too. Nadina slowly opened the door. The two men walked into the apartment. The one with the peppered hair spoke. "My name is Lien Tenant Marshall Ormonds." "We're here about the murder that took place here about a month ago." "It involved your mother who was the victim wasn't she?" Nadina stood silent. She didn't know if she could continue with the questioning with the police.

There was another knock at the door. "Who is it!" Nadina hurried to the door and flung it open. It was Herbert and she was glad to see him. He came and stood beside her. Herbert spoke to the two police officers. Lt. Redmonds spoke softly. "We're here to ask you if you've seen your mother and father, Miss Welling." "No, but if I do, I'm going to kill him," Redmond," Nadina hissed.   Lt. Redmond again spoke "NO Miss Wellings. We don't want you to do anything." You must call us." "We will take matters from there. He will answer for the horrible things he's done."

Lt. Redmonds also stated "He seems to be pretty violent, so that makes him armed and dangerous." Lt. Redmonds handed Nadina his card.

"I hope that you call Miss Wellings." Herbert said that he would call if he saw him. The two men left Nadina's apartment. Herbert still muddled about. He wanted to be sure Nadina and Remiah would be alright.

Shots then rang out in the street. Shots were heard being returned. More police came, sirens and vehicles lights blaring. "I got one of the policemen yelled at." Crowds gathered and began yelling and cursing. Why don't you go to them White towns and get some of them white people over there?" One of the black young males yelled at the police. Fearing a riot was about to erupt in the area, three of the policemen began to disperse the crowd.

"Alright, alright, break it up before it gets rough, and arrests will be made." The police began to dispense the crowd. The police began to draw the nightsticks and mace. They had to put down this insurrection or it could get worse and there would be injuries or loss of life. This area was becoming a highly volatile region. Nadina's phone in her apartment rang. It was her neighbor Millie Mae. She asked: "What's happening outside?"

Nadina said, "Some gangbangers came running over here and got more than what they bargained for." "I think it was Cordell

Makelin and his crew." "Why don't they do something else with their lives." Millie Mae wondered. Suppose they could do something with their lives if they wanted to." Nadina said with spite in their voice.

It was painful for her to remember while back when she had been sneaking around with Elton Sanders behind her mother's back. She became abandoned by her young lover. She was jerked back to the present moment when Millie Mae asked in a loud voice "you still there, girl?" After yet another round of deadly shootings in The Brighton Avenue Apartments the tally was totaled. Cordell was shot dead as were two of his friends. Winston Collins or W.C. as he was widely known as, was the only survivor of the deadly carnage. Everyone was coming at the policemen with questions. WC'S fate was sealed as was every other young black male in Evansville. Young black males were getting shot dead in the streets or being shot dead in the streets or being housed in the Evansville Penitentiary System.

Nadina was feeling a little blue after talking with Millie Mae. Sometimes she wished she had someone her own age to talk with. Most of the other girls her age were stuck up and single. Once a girl in the neighborhood became a single parent, she was ostracized as the other mothers made sure their daughters weren't infected with the rebellion and foolishness that was manifested in that rebellion.

The exclusion was really designed to solidify the social group's social circle. The young men usually preyed upon such loneliness of the women. They usually are satisfied with their lustful desires. The men usually left when the babies came. Nadina, who was already hurt and wounded emotionally by such selfish behavior, refused to allow herself to be a victim to this behavior often. Other girls who wanted to be spiritual got back at the women by carrying affairs with their husbands and bearing illegitimate children to the husbands of the women. This tactic destroyed some of the marriages. Many of the marriages stayed intact because many of the women didn't want to be subject to gossip themselves. Herbert was late for dinner again. His wife was beginning to complain.

Nadina quietly opened the door. Nadina said to Justine: "He'll be home soon. You know he works late, sometimes?" Justine screamed: "Where is that man?" "He'd better not be out with no damn bitch!" Nadina said nothing. Justine wanted no confrontation. She didn't want to get into a fight with the angry woman. Justine rolled up her eyes. Nadina flashed a quick smile at the woman. Nadina flashed a quick smile at Justine who was still angry and getting more angrier by the minute.

Another door opened and MIllie Mae stuck her head out of the door of her apartment. "Hi, how are you folks getting along?" "Justine." "I'll be fine when that man of mine gets home!" Justine sounded as if she was aspiring. Nadina: "Millie Mae, maybe he's working late again." Maybe he's out there noisin' in what's goin' on in the streets like he always does." Millie Mae then laughed. Justine: "Millie Mae, if you don't shut yo' ol' gray mouth……..." Before Millie Mae could reply the doors to the elevator opened and Herbert stepped out. "Y'all see what's goin' on out there." "Cordell is dead and some of his buddies are too." "They say only one of 'em was left alive." Pauline Davis (Cordell's mother) "Lord Jesus!" Justine screaming: "Oh my God, poor Pauline!" The year before Pauline lost her youngest son (Melvin) in gang violence. Now her eldest son is gone in a police shooting. The complex was being rocked by one problem after another. Millie Mae: "Justine was worried about you Herbert." Herbert looked at his wife. He mumbled something and went into his apartment. Justine followed her husband. Millie Mae: "It's so hard on everybody. "When the boys are killed like that," "Cordell was stupid, anyway. How else did he expect to end up?"

Two weeks went by. Amidst the angst of news reports about the shootings and the funerals that followed, there was very little to be happy about. Herbert was talking about the shootings and attending the funerals. He had known Cordell's mother in more than just a casual way. Many joked behind Herbert's back that Pauline's youngest son was his. He denied anything that was said to his face.

Even though it was rumored that Herbert got around with the women. No one wanted to fool around with Herbert and his issues. Six months went by. After a cooling off period, gang wars resumed themselves for top positions in the street. People usually went out during the day for their affairs and barricaded themselves. Anyone outside after eight o'clock at night usually regretted it. People were attacked for their purses, wallets, or anything else of value. Most of the time, the criminals were caught. Other times there was a long time before they (the criminals, that is) were caught. At that time, the residents of Brighton Avenue quietly rejoiced. Times got better and things were quieter. Then the vicious process would start all over again.

Arletta and Nadina were fast becoming friends. The hardships were becoming easier to bear as the two women began to help each other. The Evansville County Social Services System each assisted the young women. It was easier for Nadina because of the fact that she had a daughter. It was different for Arletta because she was single. The Evansville County Social Services System expected Arletta to go to school or to work. Nadina wondered what it would be like to get a high school diploma.

So at the age of eighteen, she had decided to go back to school. "Want some company, Ketta?" (A nickname that Nadina had given her new friend.) "I don't care cause I'm droppin' out anyway when I get my check," Arletta said flippantly. Then what cha' gonna do after that?" Nadina chuckled to her new friend.

Nadina already knew the answer. She knew she could count on her friend to stay in school for a while anyway. Nadina found a sitter for Remiah, who had a fit because she didn't like being away from her mother. Nadina was the more "smarter" one and helped Arletta with homework often. Arletta would get into fights every so often when she was picked on at school. Nadina came pretty close to having a couple of encounters herself. Nonetheless, they both struggled through the difficult day.

A year after Nadina's mother's death, there was a knock at her door. It was two detectives. Det. Morton Collier and Det. Colton Hanson came to see Nadina. It was the worst day of her life. They announced that they had caught her father in a small town earlier in Jasper, Miss. He was held without bail in Jasper, and that he was to be extradited back to Evansville to stand trial for her mother's murder.

When the detectives left, Nadina's phone started ringing. Nadina didn't want to talk to anyone and yet, everyone wanted to know about her father's capture. It was Milie Mae who came over to Nadina's apartment to see what she could do to help the beleaguered young woman. Remiah was playing on the floor with her black Barbie Doll. Millie Mae took some of the calls ringing from Nadina's phone.

They were from nosy neighbors who wanted to know about Nadina's father and the trial. The day dragged into night and the laughter talking among the women and Remiah hurried the early evening into late night. Nadina announced that she was taking the phone off the cradle all night. Arletta hated to go but Millie Mae was scolding her about getting up and going to school. Both Nadina and Arletta were getting more than annoyed at Millie Mae even though she was right.

Two weeks later, Nadina's father was brought back to the Evansville County Jail. He asked repeatedly, to see Nadina. She refused and took no more calls from him. He attempted to write, but his handwriting was illegible, and difficult to read. Nadina wanted the whole matter to be over. Remiah was told not to talk about her grandfather. She was also told not to refer to him as "grandfather." Herbert paid a visit to Nadina's apartment on Wednesday.

It was a cool balmy day in August in the late afternoon. Nineteen eighty-four was an unusual violent year for Evansville. The deaths were mounting and the police had their hands full with suspects shootings and gangs fighting over turf and areas of the city they considered their own.

Herbert was helpful to Nadina although he used Nadina's vulnerability to get closer to Arletta. Arletta had now considered herself a friend to Nadina and had adopted herself to Remiah as her aunt. Herbert had the hots for Arletta and was relentless in his pursuit of her. Millie Mae and Nadina were just as relentless in keeping the married man and single girl apart. Arletta enjoyed the attention and playfulness that Herbert was bestowing on her. Justine worked and did not suspect the fact that Herbert's roving eyes had settled on Millie Mae's niece. Problems would multiply as both Arletta and Nadina's lives would spiral out of control with tragic consequences.

Two years had passed. It was the spring of nineteen-eighty-six. The sun was melting all the ice and snow the preceding brutal winter had left behind in Evansville. Nadina's father was now being put on trial for the murder of her mother. Most of Evansville's black community attended the court proceedings, and shouted obscenities at WIllie Wellings.

As the trial proceeded, Willie's public defender lawyer attempted to question a few witnesses trying to gain some ground for his defendant. The trial was a problem from the start. Not only did most of the neighborhood hated Willie, but they hated him much more for killing Lena. The trial dragged on for a month.

WIllie shouted in the courtroom that he was Nadina's father and that he loved her. Nadina and Remiah ran from the courtroom with Nadina in tears. After a month, with all the evidence and testimony from witnesses, the twelve jury panel found Willie Wellings guilty of 1st degree manslaughter. Nadina demanded to know why her father wasn't found guilty of murder. "Nadina talked to Wanda Pennigton, one of the jurors of the trail."

Mrs. Pennigton was a heavy-set and light-skinned balck woman who was afraid to speak her mind. "They were arguing and he lost his temper." That wasn't 1st degree murder, he was just a fool who lost his cool. He'll still pay for it." Nadina still turned and ran from pursuit. "Wait, mama, wait, for me." Remiah shouted at the distraught young woman.

Nadina cried all day. It was a cold October day, made even colder by what she thought was a miscarrage of justice. Thanksgiving Day, nineteen eighty-seven, brought little source of comfort for Nadina who was sentenced from ten to fifteen years in the Evansville State Penitentiary. For a while, Nadina's father tried to call her and when she would answer him, he quit calling. Willie died in a prison fight six months after his incarceration for Lena's Killing. Nadina wondered whether she could have talked to him before he died. She refused to attend his funeral. He was shipped to Jasper, Miss, where he had been born.

Two of his brothers were well off and paid for his services. Nadina had stopped being so bitter after his death. She turned to Millie Mae and Arletta for comfort and support. Several months had passed. The holidays in particular Christmas, nineteen eighty-eight, had been bleak and Nadina did all she could to make the holiday a bright one for Remiah. Hebert and Justice had brought her a new black Barbie doll, plus other gifts. The small get together in the couple's apartment had given Nadina and Remiah a small sense of comfort.

"I invited Arletta and Millie Mae to the Christmas Dinner. Why didn't they come?" Hebert asked Nadina (as they were standing in a quiet corner of the house)``"You know the answer to that, Nadina answered coldly." "That's the way you talk to me, after I help you out?" Herbert hissed quietly at Nadina. Just then, Justine came back into the room. Herbert retreated to the kitchen. Nadina walked up to Justice.

"Nice dinner party," she said to Justice smiling at the woman. "Really?" Justice asked as his eyes snapped with anger. "You don't think that Herbert and I …." Nadina's voice trailed off. The growing friendship between Nadina and Arletta was giving a measure of source and comfort to Nadina and Remiah was thrilled with having an "Aunt." It was still tricky to keep Herbert and Arletta apart; Arletta wasn't particularly interested in Herbert but enjoyed the attention Hebert was lavishing on her.

On a warm spring-like April afternoon, Bea stopped by. Nadina was shocked to see a pregnant Bea in front of her when she opened the door to her apartment. "Hello, Nadina." "Are you busy, can we come in?" Bea asked Jokingly. "Yeah, sure," Nadina replied, staring at her mother's friend with a puzzled look on her face.

She walked past Nadina and sat down on the couch in the living room. Remiah, hearing the front door opening, came running out of her bedroom to see who it was visiting her and her mother. When Bea saw Remiah she spoke to her and remarked how tall she was getting. Nadina asked her the "question." "Who's the baby's father," Nadina asked. Bea, she smiled and said nothing. "Who's the baby's father?" Remiah asked.

Again, Bea smiled. Although she did not say anything, Nadina suspected a certain ladies man within the building. Nadina hoped that Justine wouldn't find out about Herbert's latest extracurricular activities. A knock at the door occurred again. A knock at the door occurred again. Ndina got up and went to the door. After she peeped through the small hole in the door, she swung it wide open. Arletta stood in the doorway grinning.

"What's up, girl?" she laughed as she came through the door. As she caught sight of Bea, she stopped. "Oh, I didn't know you had company, Nadina," Arletta said. "I was just leaving," Bea retorted flippantly. It was evident that she didn't like Arletta. Nadina was glad that Bea was leaving because she preferred Arletta's company.

She needed to find out about Lionel Gibbons being shot and who did the shooting. She also had something to say about Bea. "I thought she'd never leave," Nadina said to Arletta as she closed the door behind her. "I hate the fact that she comes over here," Nadina said, the disgust evident in her voice. "Wonder why she comes," Arletta sneered. "She's pregnant, isn't she?" Arletta asked Nadina. "Oh sure. She just came over here to rub it in your face." "I think that the baby's daddy is Herbert." Arletta's brown eyes flickered with anger. "You think I care whose baby that bitch is pregnant with?" She said flippantly to Nadina. "Well, if you're going to……," Nadina started to say. "I came here to see you anyway, not to talk about anybody," Arletta said, cutting off Nadina's sentence.

The young women continued on with their conversations and talked about Bea soon ceased. Laughter was heard in the hallway followed by loud yelling. The yelling soon turned to cuss words and threats of killing. Nadina and Arletta ran to the door to put their ears to Nadina's front room door. The yelling by two women went on. "You are just no good, you nasty whore!" One woman shouted at the other. "You wouldn't know what's good or bad is because you're not that intelligent," the second woman responded.

Nadina slowly opened the door from her apartment. She saw a pregnant Bea arguing with another woman. The other big heavy-set woman grabbed Bea and began pushing her. Nadina raced up the hall and grabbed the heavy-set woman. Arletta gently held on to

Bea. Arletta gently walked Bea back to Nadina's apartment. Nadina told the heavy-set woman to go back to her apartment or the police would come and take her away. As she was being led back to Nadina's apartment, Bea looked glib. Arletta suddenly resented the pregnant woman.

"What are you looking at?" Bea asked Arletta.

"Nothin' I wanna look at," Arletta replied flippantly.

As Nadina opened the door to her apartment she wished Bea would keep quiet before she would have to break up a fight between the girl and the woman. The women went into Nadina's apartment and sat down in the living room on the sofa. Arletta suddenly stood up and decided to leave. "Arletta, where you goin' girl?" Nadina asked. "I just remembered my Aunt Millie Mae had somethin' for me to do." Arletta replied coldly.

Arletta hurried to the front door-opened it, and slammed the door behind her as she walked across the hall to her aunt's apartment. Nadina was frustrated as she looked at Bea wondering what to say to her. Bea smiled smugly as if she was happy that Arletta was gone. It made Nadina angry. She suddenly snapped at Bea. "Don't sit there looking so smug. Secrets get around here a lot. If you think you can hide what you did, you've got another thought coming!" Nadina snapped at the woman. "What are you talking about, Nadina?" Bea asked.

Nadina was even more furious. "Never mind, you treacherous……." Nadina hissed. "Guess I'd better be on my way," Bea said. "Yeah, I've got things to do as well." Nadina snapped verbally at the woman who was annoying her to no end. Bea struggled to get up from the couch. She was with child and Nadina made no attempts to assist the pregnant woman. Bea waddled to the front door, opened it, and walked out. This time, Nadina would not interrupt any disturbance she may run into. At the same time, she hoped Bea would make it out the door to the street without a problem.

Bea went to the door, opened it, and left Nadina's apartment. As Nadina listened to the sound of Bea's footsteps going down the hall to the elevator. When Nadina heard the elevator doors close, she was happy that Bea left her apartment and the building. Remiah came into the living room. "Will Aunt Bea come back, Mama?" She asked. "I hope not, she's so much trouble." Nadina replied calmly.

Nadina and her sister would get ready for the tough future that they faced without their mother. They were not ready for what the future held for them. But they were willing to face whatever obstacles that they had to face and the lot in life that they had. They were willing to face the fact that their mother was not coming home, and were willing to deal with the challenges and difficulties that were ahead of them as a family.